# MUNCH

Written and
illustrated by
**Emma McCann**

Albury Books

The alarm clock went off...
DRING! DRING!

...just as MUNCH was enjoying
a very nice dream about toast
and coconut jam.

Dragging himself out of bed,
he went to the kitchen to
have breakfast.

He was just munching his way through his 17 slices of toast with banana jam, when something caught his eye in the newspaper.

# WIBBLE DAILY NEWS

## GIANT MONSTER GOES RAVENOUS RAMPA

**This picture taken by a reader some fear to be the enormous**

An enormous monster caused chaos in Wibble town centre yesterday as it ate its way through hundreds of houses. Terrified homeowners watched in horror as the huge creature swallowed down several streets, leaving many monsters homeless, before

crunch cars fo Nobo plan com has pla fea st v

"GOOD GRIEF!" exclaimed MUNCH out loud, dropping his toast on the floor. "Maybe I should stay home and protect my house from being eaten!"

MUNCH sat up all day,

The same evening over **11** slices of toast with broccoli jam, MUNCH put on the television.

The news was on and something caught his eye.

The **enormous** monster that MUNCH had seen in the newspaper was on the television gulping down **trees** and \amposts and buses and anything else it could fit in its gigantic mouth.

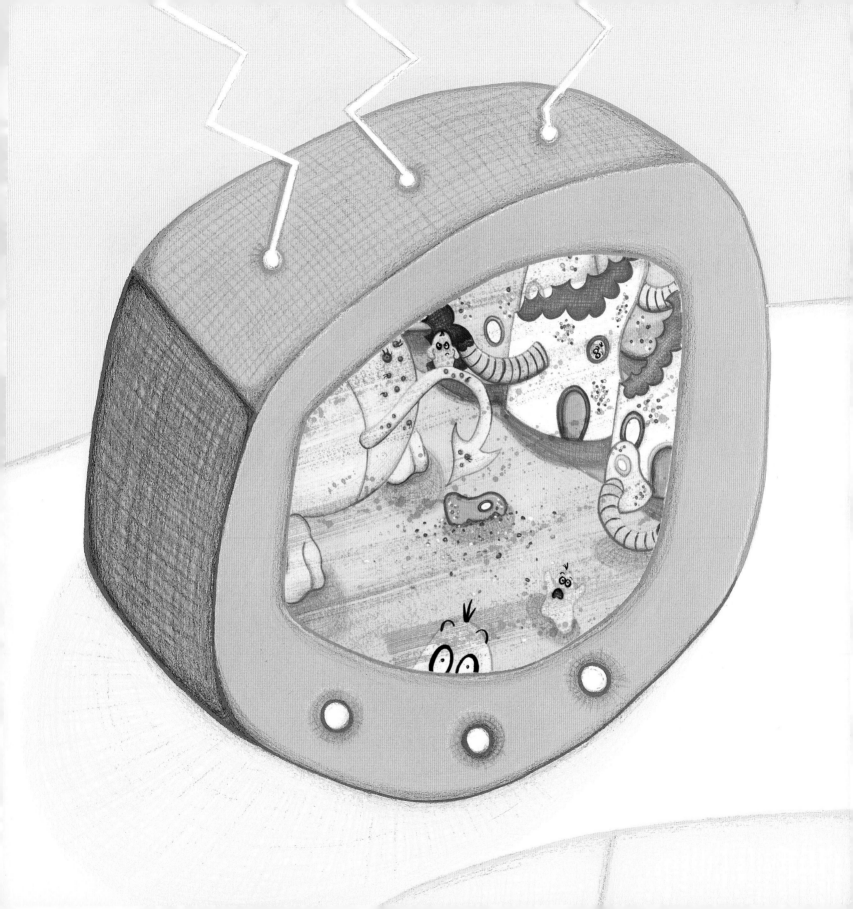

and all day.

But no **enormous** monster came.

# "WHERE'S MY TOASTER?"

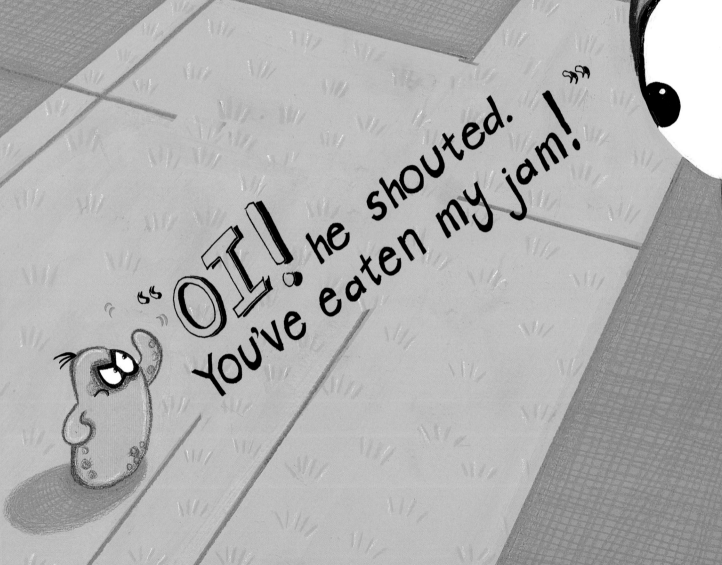

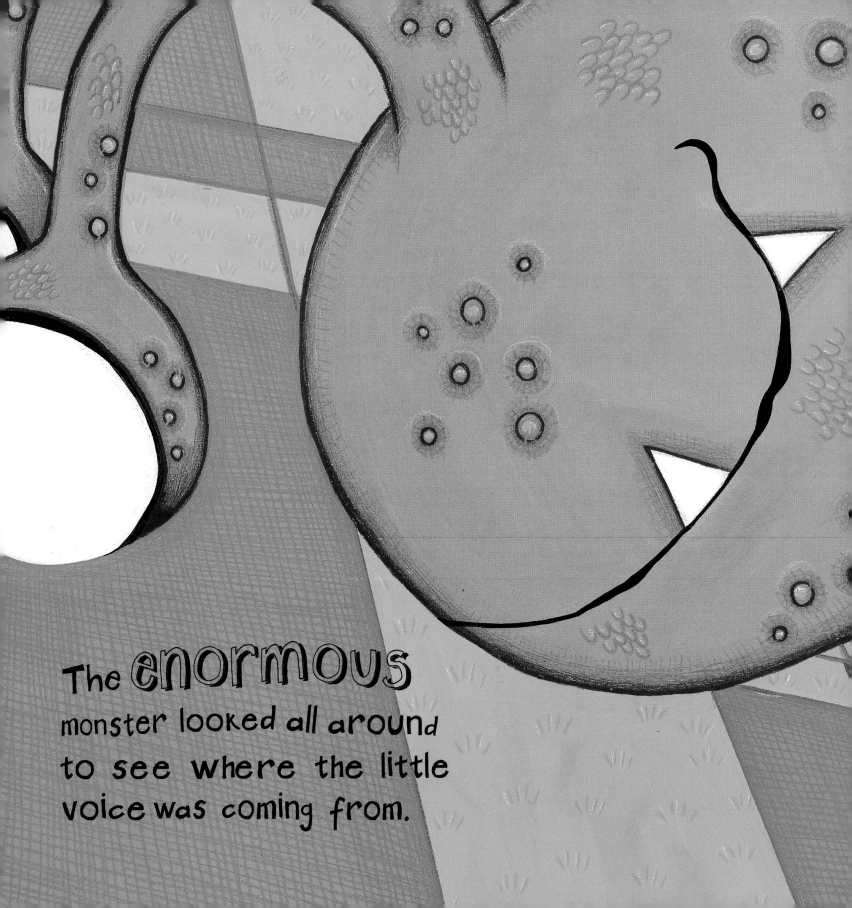

The **enormous** monster looked all around to see where the little voice was coming from.

It saw MUNCH'S angry face and started to laugh.

And the more it laughed, the angrier MUNCH became.

The enormous monster came closer and closer licking its lips.

It bent down,

opened its mouth and...

nch!

# MUNCH swallowed him up instead.

Pity he had no jam.

For Muvver and Spud
E.M.

Even if one prefers Lemon Curd and the other doesn't like toast.

Munch
Text Copyright © Em McCann | Illustration Copyright © Emma McCann

The rights of Emma McCann to be identified as the author and illustrator
have been asserted by them in accordance with the Copyright, Designs and
Patents Act, 1988

Published in 2016 by Albury Books
Albury Court, Albury, Oxfordshire, OX9 2LP

www.AlburyBooks.com

A CIP catalogue record for this book is available
from the British Library

978-1-910235-11-9

Printed in China